T0370502

Is Frank Finally Home?

AuthorHouse™
1663 Liberty Drive
Bloomington, IN 47403
www.authorhouse.com
Phone: 1 (800) 839-8640

Published by AuthorHouse 04/20/2018

ISBN: 978-1-5462-3702-0 (sc)
ISBN: 978-1-5462-3703-7 (e)

Library of Congress Control Number: 2018904290

Print information available on the last page.

authorHOUSE®

The Kids of Nettleton

Is Frank Finally Home?

Book 2

March 2018

Written & Illustrated

by

Micma

This book is dedicated to Frank Goodale

Many, many thanks to Frank for making this book possible. Thank you for answering my endless questions, for allowing me access to your memory bank, for having the patience to assist me with the smallest of historical details. Thank you, my friend.

Micma

CHAPTERS

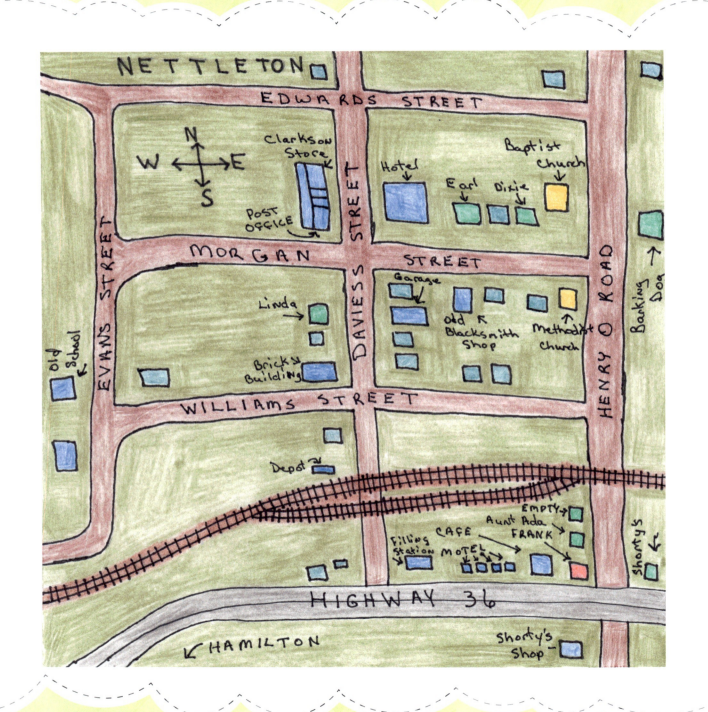

Chapter One

Frank's Chore

July 1952

Frank moved the glass jar from one arm to the other. He only had to carry it about three blocks to Clarkson's store, but it was already feeling heavy. His mom needed oil for the cookstove, and Frank had assured her he could do this chore. After all, he would be seven-years-old next week. Plus, he was the man of the house.

Looking both directions for a train like his mom had taught him, he crossed the railroad tracks. Between the churches, at Morgan Street, Frank turned left. Down the block, he could see a couple of older boys in front of a house. He crossed to the other side of the road to avoid them.

Frank, his mom, his sister, and his brother had moved to Nettleton just last week. He had met only a few of the townspeople.

Frank kept his head straight and his eyes on his goal, Clarkson's store, as he passed the old blacksmith shop across the street from the older boys. Maybe they wouldn't notice him.

He was in luck; they hadn't seen him. He crossed the road on the far side of the intersection, walked by the post office and entered the store. Bung was behind the counter.

"Hello," Bung smiled. "What have you got there?" Nathan and Francis Clarkson own the store, but Frank had learned on his first visit to the store to call Francis by her nickname, Bung.

Frank heaved the gallon jar onto the counter. "Mom needs coal oil for the cookstove, please." Frank shook his arms, getting his circulation to return. *Whew!* What a relief.

Nathan came to the counter to retrieve the jar and take it to the back of the store where he kept the kerosene.

"How are you kids and your mom settling in?" Bung asked, leaning over the counter to be level with Frank.

"Pretty good," Frank answered. "We have a kitchen table and four chairs now!" He glanced around the store. There were a couple of men behind him sitting in chairs around an unlit coal stove, talking. He hadn't seen them here on his previous trips to the store. The big guy was wearing overalls and had a cane leaning against his knee. The other man was talking about the corn crops.

"That's good to hear," Bung nodded. "Have you made some friends?"

"Well, just Shorty's family," Frank replied, "but they are all girls."

Bung chuckled. "Don't worry; there are boys in Nettleton, too. Manley over there," she gestured to indicate the man with the cane, "has a son a couple of years older than you."

"Really?" Frank smiled. It was actually a relief to hear there really were boys closer to his age living in Nettleton. Frank had seen older boys entering and leaving the café next to his house. He'd noticed girls riding bikes around town. The only kids he had seen about his size had been girls.

Nathan approached carrying the jar filled with oil. He set it by Frank's feet.

"The bottle is a little heavy," he told Frank. "You sure you can handle carrying it all the way home?"

Frank stood up as tall as possible. "Yes, sir."

Nathan chuckled. "I reckon you'll do fine. Tell your mom we'll put it on her account."

"I will." Frank hoisted the jar with both arms. "Thank you."

Outside, he crossed the parking lot. At the sidewalk by the hotel he had to set the jar down to rest his arms. As he lifted the jar again, he thought, *Maybe I should ask Santa for a wagon at Christmas.* They had room for a wagon now. They had a big yard and plenty of space in the house.

He focused on the long stretch of sidewalk on this block. He had quite a way to go, then another two blocks after he turned at the corner.

He caught sight of a movement out of the corner of his eye. *Uh, oh!* He had forgotten about the two boys. They were still outside at the next house, and Frank was on their side of the street.

Picking up the jar, he walked past the big hotel. He hoped he wouldn't need to rest again until after he was beyond their house. He tried but he couldn't make it any farther. He set the oil down.

"Hey," one of them called as they both started walking in Frank's direction. "What do you have there?"

"Um," Frank stammered nervously.

"Your family moved in down by the highway, right?" asked the red-headed boy.

Frank nodded.

"I'm Leon," said the other boy, then pointed to his friend. "That's Earl."

"I'm Frank. We moved in last week." His nervousness was easing up a bit. "Is this your house?"

"It's mine," Earl told him. "But we're moving soon. See that house over that way?" He pointed to the west. "You can't see all of it. Mostly the roof."

Frank looked. The house Earl was pointing at was maybe a block and a half away. He nodded.

"My dad is getting that house ready for us to move into in a few weeks," Earl continued. "A couple of years ago it was our school here in Nettleton. Now we ride the bus to Hamilton for school."

"Are you going to school this year?" Leon asked him.

Frank nodded, again. "I'll be in first grade."

"We're going to be in third grade," Leon told him.

Frank looked from one boy to the other. "Are you twins?" Frank knew not all twins looked alike.

Both boys started laughing.

"No," Leon told him. "We're best friends. I live on the other side of the highway beyond Earl's new house."

"Oh," Frank was a little embarrassed. He picked up the oil jar. "I better get home. My mom will need this to cook dinner. Nice to meet you." He nodded good-bye, as his arms were full.

"We'll see you around," they told him as they watched him lug the heavy jar down the sidewalk.

The big house at the end of the road had a dog. He barked as Frank approached the corner. Frank didn't know what he would do if he had to outrun the dog. The oil was heavy. He sure didn't want to drop and break Mom's cook stove bottle.

The dog continued to bark until Frank was almost to the tracks at the end of the block. *At least it didn't leave the yard*, Frank thought.

Frank walked past the empty house by the tracks. He rested again in front of the next house. After setting the jar on the ground, he used his arm to brush away the sweat on his forehead. Almost home.

Two rest stops later, Frank placed the jar beside the cook stove in the kitchen.

"What a big boy you are," his mom gave him a big hug. "Thank you for getting this for me."

"It was no problem," Frank assured her. He sat at the table with a glass of water. It was turning into a typical hot July day outside. Lugging the heavy jar three blocks had made him sweat like crazy. "Nathan said to tell you he put it on your account."

"That's fine."

Frank's little brother, Jim, tried to climb onto his lap. "Stay down, Jim," he pushed him away. "I'm hot."

However, when a two-year-old wants to sit on your lap, he can be very persistent. Frank handed Jim the rest of his water to distract him.

"Mom," Frank said, "I met a couple of boys. They are older, a little, but I think they are nice."

"Were they at the store, too?" Mom attached the jar to the cookstove, and then stood upright, reaching around to rub her lower back. Mom is six months pregnant. She must be careful not to lift heavy stuff.

"No," Frank shook his head. "They were in the yard at Earl's house. But…"

The front door opened, interrupting Frank. Their Uncle Lindy walked in, coming through the living room to the kitchen to sit at the table with Frank.

"Uncle Lindy!" Ardell, Frank's little sister, squealed. She followed their uncle into the kitchen and jumped onto his lap, hugging him.

"Hello, Pumpkin," Uncle Lindy kissed Ardell's cheek. He pulled Jim onto his other knee, giving him a little squeeze.

"How's it going with you?" he asked Frank. "Are you making friends?"

"We were just talking about that," Evelyn told her brother, setting a glass of water on the table in front of him. She placed her hand on Frank's shoulder. "Frank met a couple of new friends today."

"You don't say!"

Frank nodded. "Earl and Leon. Earl lives in the house by the big hotel, but he's moving soon. He's moving to the old schoolhouse over that way," Frank pointed out the back door to the west.

Uncle Lindy glanced at Frank's mom. "You don't say," he repeated, thoughtfully.

Ardell giggled. "You already said that."

Uncle Lindy tickled her, grinning. "You don't say."

Chapter Two

Frank Goes Exploring

For the rest of the week, Frank walked around Nettleton. The town was small, having only a few blocks, but he met several new people.

Ada, or Aunt Ada, as she told Frank to call her, lives two houses north of Frank. Out of her seven kids, only Jack and Sam, both teenagers, still live with her. Her five oldest kids have moved away and have families of their own. She works in her big garden every day. His little sister, Ardell, likes to visit Aunt Ada. Frank learned that Aunt Ada's parents, the Goins, run the big hotel.

After Aunt Ada's house, heading north, is the empty house, then the railroad tracks. The train usually comes through three times a day but more often on some days. The rail cars carry big crates, U.S. mail, smelly livestock, and many passengers. The rails run from Hannibal to Saint Joseph.

The Methodist Church is at the end of the next block, with the Baptist Church on the other side of Morgan Street. Frank counted a dozen houses he could see while standing on that corner. He didn't know any of the residents, but he looked forward to meeting them. That dog started barking again, inspiring Frank not to linger there for long.

As he passed the house behind the Methodist Church, he saw a woman in the back yard working in her garden. At the next house, a man was carrying a bag into the shed behind his house. Toys and bikes were scattered in several yards.

He walked down the sidewalk towards Earl's house. He was hoping Earl would be outside, but no such luck. He continued making his way around the blocks.

Around the corner south of Clarkson's was an automotive garage. The big door was open. A man was leaning over an engine under the hood of a car. Two men were sitting on stools near the workbench along the wall. Frank could hear them talking, but he couldn't make out the words.

He crossed the street to look in the windows of the big brick building. He cupped his hands around his eyes to block the light. It is a feed store.

"Hey," he heard a boy shout. Frank lowered his hands, jumping back from the window.

The boy was running up the sidewalk. He stopped beside Frank, breathing hard. "I'm Wayne. What are you looking at in there?"

"Nothing," Frank hoped he wasn't in trouble for being nosy or curious. "I just wondered what was in the building."

"That's a feed store," Wayne told him. "But they use the building for all sorts of things. Like parties, dances, and meetings. You name it."

"Hmm," Frank looked in the window again. "I'm Frank, by the way."

"Yep, I know," Wayne told him. "I've heard all about you. Hey, I'm heading down to the café on the highway. Do you want to come with me?"

"I guess." Frank turned away from the window to walk beside him. "How do you know about me?"

"Bung, Nathan, Earl, Leon. They've all mentioned you." Wayne shrugged his shoulders, as though talking about the new boy in town was no big deal.

They crossed the tracks, then cut through the yard behind a filling station.

"My mom is at Clarkson's," Wayne informed him. "While she does her shopping, I like to watch the older boys play on the new pinball machine at the café. Do you play pinball?"

Frank shook his head.

"Me, either. Not very often, anyways," Wayne told him. "I don't have any money. But when we come to town, Mom lets me run down here and watch. It's fun."

"You don't live in town?"

"Nah," Wayne answered as they walked behind the motel rooms and carport. "I live a mile or so over that way," he pointed south.

The Conoco Station was actually several businesses in one. Running parallel with Highway 36 were the motel rooms and carport the boys had walked behind. In front of the main building were two gas pumps. The room where they entered had a counter with a cash register and some racks holding potato chip bags and automotive odds and ends. The café was in the back with a counter and stools, a few tables and the pinball machine.

At the pinball machine, an older boy was playing a game. Another boy was watching, leaving room for Frank and Wayne to stand on the other side.

Frank recognized Jack, Aunt Ada's son. Jack was the one playing while his friend watched. He was good at playing pinball. Wayne told him the other boy was Pete.

When Jack finished his game, he offered to let them play a game.

"We don't have any money," Frank told him. "We'll watch if you are playing another game."

The waitress, a girl named Barbara, came over to ask them if they needed anything.

"Can I get you boys a drink, maybe a sandwich?"

"No, thanks," Wayne told her, "we're just watching."

Pete moved away to talk to Barbara for a minute until her mom called her back to the counter.

"There's no time for that, young lady," Frank heard Barbara's mom scold her. "You take that couple their food and quit your flirting!"

"Oh, Mom!" Barbara rolled her eyes, but she picked up the plates and delivered them to the waiting couple.

The older boys had played three more games before Wayne's mom came to pick him up on her way home. Frank left for his house located next door. He had explored most of two blocks today, which had taken a while. He should probably be getting home before his mom started worrying.

Frank was feeling good as he crossed the yard. He had only lived in Nettleton two weeks, and he already had many new friends. Now his friends were Leon, Earl, Wayne, Donna, Sandra, and even Aunt Ada, Nathan and Bung. Possibly the two boys playing pinball, also, Jack and Pete. Maybe in the morning when they went to church, he would meet even more new friends.

Chapter Three

Time for Church

Sunday morning Frank's family walked to the Methodist Church two blocks north of their house. Mom held Ardell's hand while Jim ran ahead. Shorty's family was behind them. Aunt Ada and her son's stepped out of their house and walked the same direction. Mom grabbed Jim's hand before they crossed the tracks. The church was ahead on the left.

The church wasn't too big. Soon every pew was filled. Frank hadn't realized Nettleton had so many residents, especially kids. He wondered if any of these people lived in the houses he'd seen yesterday.

The preacher began the service with a greeting to the congregation. Next, he invited everyone to welcome the newcomers, which were Frank's family. Frank could feel his face turn red when everyone in the church turned to look at his family. Some of the people murmured hellos. Then they said a prayer. The congregation stood as they sang a hymn while a woman named Eleanor played the piano.

Once they were seated, the preacher resumed his place at the podium. He instructed the kids to line up at the door and follow Mrs. Teegarden to the Baptist Church.

"Mom?" Frank looked at his mom for permission, not sure if he should leave her or not.

"It's all right," Mom patted him on the knee. "The Baptist Church is across the street. You will come back here after class for the sermon."

Frank and Ardell joined the other kids in line. Jim was too young, so he stayed with their mom. The youngsters met a group of older kids heading toward the Methodist Church.

The Baptist Church had a big bell mounted on cement piers. He vaguely remembered hearing it ring right before the preacher had started talking. He hoped he remembered to listen for it next Sunday.

Inside, this church was bigger than the Methodist Church. Frank was led to an area with Earl, Leon, Wayne, Donna, Sandra and two other girls. Already sitting around their teacher were a few more kids who must be members of this church. Their teacher's name was Beulah Faye.

"Today's lesson is about Moses as a baby," said Beulah Faye.

"We have a baby," said Sandra.

Her sister, Donna, nodded. "She's little. You have to be very careful with her."

"We have Baby Sam," said Earl. "He's this big." Earl spread his hands from shoulder to shoulder.

"My mom is going to have a baby," Frank told them. "But not yet. We have to wait some more."

Beulah Faye smiled. "Well, this baby, Baby Moses, was the first-born son of a Hebrew family. But the Pharaoh had learned that a baby boy had been born, a first son of a Hebrew family, that would someday grow up to challenge the Pharaoh. The Pharaoh got scared. He ordered his men to kill every first-born son in every Hebrew family."

"That's awful," Donna cried out.

"He's a mean man," said Wayne.

"Yes," Beulah Faye nodded. "Mean and scared and selfish." She continued with her story. "The Hebrews heard what he was planning, and they were scared, too."

"What did they do?" Frank asked.

"Well," Beulah Faye told them, "Moses' mom placed him in a woven basket and hid the basket in the reeds at the river. She had Moses' big sister stay near him, but out of sight, to watch over him. But then the sister ran home to tell her mom the news."

"What news?" the kids asked.

"Why would she leave her baby brother all alone?" asked Donna.

Beulah Faye held up her finger, indicating for them to wait, the story wasn't finished. "She rushed home to tell her mom that the Pharaoh's sister had found Moses and decided to keep the little Hebrew baby to raise as her own son."

"She can't do that!" Earl said, sounding angry. "He's not her baby."

"Oh, but she can," Beulah Faye told them. "The Egyptians were in charge, and the Hebrews only slaves."

"But Moses will miss his mom," said Martha.

"Yes," their teacher nodded. "And his mom missed him. Very much. But if she tried to get Moses back from the Pharaoh's sister, the Pharaoh would kill him because he was her firstborn son. So, she left him with the Pharaoh's sister to be raised in the palace."

"That's cool that he got to grow up in a palace," said Leon.

"Maybe," said Patricia, "but what if he was the Hebrew baby that the Pharaoh was scared of?"

"I think we'll save the rest of the story for next week," Beulah Faye told them. "Are you ready for your snack before the sermons begin?"

They all nodded.

After their cookies and juice, Mrs. Teegarden led them back to the Methodist Church. Frank's class sat in the front pew until the preacher called on them to recite their scripture of the day.

"Start children off on the way they should go, and even when they are old they will not turn from it. Proverbs 22:6," Frank recited with the rest of his class.

After scriptures, the children could sit by their families. Frank didn't pay much attention to the sermon. He was still thinking about the baby, Moses.

On the walk home, Frank heard Ardell telling Jim about her Sunday school class. "I have lots of new friends. I met Linda and Judy. Linda lives in town. Judy lives in the country. They are coming to our house later today."

Frank turned to his mom and pointed at her belly. "Mom, no one can take our baby, can they?"

"Why, Frank, where did you get such an idea!" his mom exclaimed.

"Because that bad man's sister took Baby Moses," Frank explained.

"Oh, honey," his mom leaned down and gave him a hug. She squatted down in front of him to look him straight in the eye, her hands on his shoulders. "That was a long, long time ago. It's not like that anymore."

"Are you sure?" He was still worried.

"I'm positive," Mom said firmly. "Now no more seriousness today. We are going home to eat lunch. This afternoon your grandparents, Uncle Lindy and some of your new friends are coming over to help you eat your birthday cake."

Frank grinned, cheering up. He had almost forgotten about his party. Lunch couldn't be over fast enough!

Chapter Four

Frank's Birthday Gift

Frank looked around the room at all the people in his house. His first big birthday party! He even got a present, two guns and a holster.

His mom led the children to the backyard. They sat down in a circle to play **Duck, Duck, Goose**.

"Goose!" Earl bopped Frank on the head, taking off at a run. Frank chased him around the circle, trying to tag him before he took the spot where Frank had been

sitting. Earl plopped down, leaving Frank to be the one to choose which spot in the circle he wanted to try to win.

"Duck, duck, duck, duck," he patted each kid on the head. He was aiming for his sister or her friend Judy. There was no way either one of them could catch him. "Goose!" he yelled as he tagged his sister and took off running. She was only halfway around the circle when Frank stole her spot.

Frank thought the party was over way too soon. This had been the best birthday he could ever remember!

"Mom, can I play Roy Rogers with Earl and Leon tomorrow?" Frank asked as he helped her clean up after everyone had left.

"We'll see," his mom told him. "It's looks like it's going to rain."

"So, if it's not raining tomorrow," Frank persisted, "I can go to Earl's house?"

"Maybe," was all Mom would promise.

Frank had to decide that "maybe" was better than "no."

When they went to bed that night, it was raining cats and dogs, as Uncle Lindy would say.

Frank lay on the floor next to his mom's bed, snuggled into a layer of blankets with his sister and brother. He could hear the wind and rain.

"Let it stop," he whispered. "Let the rain stop before I wake up."

But in the morning, it was still raining!

"Oh, no!" Frank heard his mom exclaim as he sat at the table, eating his breakfast.

Frank, Ardell and Jim all ran up the stairs. *Oh, no!* they thought, too. The floors were wet from the rain and the ceiling was still leaking. Their mom was on her knees soaking up the water with rags.

"Run downstairs and bring me our bowls," she told them. Frank and Ardell ran back downstairs, but Jim started stomping in the water puddles.

"Jim, don't spread the water," Mom told him. But Jim thought splashing water with his foot was fun. Stomp, splash! Stomp, splash!

Frank handed his mom a couple of bowls. "I'm sorry, Mom."

"It's not your fault, Frank," she said as she placed bowls under the drips. "This is just an old house with a lot of problems."

"Is the rain why we have to sleep downstairs?" asked Ardell.

"Partially." Mom went back to mopping up the water. "I didn't know about the leaky roof until this morning. This is our first rain since moving here. Mostly it's hot up here. You don't want to get sweaty while you're sleeping, right?" The kids shook their heads.

Little Jim was disappointed when Mom had all the puddles dried and they went back downstairs. They could hear the drips hitting the metal bowls from the kitchen.

Frank was disappointed, too. He wouldn't get to play with his friends today after all.

He loaned his sister one of his guns, and they ran around the house shooting imaginary bad men. But Ardell slid on the rug and fell against the books stacked in the living room. Almost one whole wall was covered with stacks of books that belonged to Shorty.

Shorty lives across the street to the east. He operates an outdoor ornament shop across the highway to the south. He had been using this house for storage when Frank's family moved in. Some of his stuff was still here including his books.

Luckily, only one stack of books fell, but a couple hit Ardell on her back. Mom came running in from the kitchen when she heard the books hit the floor and Ardell's crying.

"It's all right," Mom gathered Ardell in her arms and rocked her. "It's going to be all right."

Ardell's crying dwindled to sniffles.

Frank tried to stack the books back where they belonged, but he wasn't tall enough.

"I'll get that," Mom told him. "You kids go on, now."

By Wednesday, the mud from the rain had mostly dried up. Mom allowed Frank to walk to Earl's house but only if he took his sister with him.

"You can't play guns with us," Frank told Ardell as they walked.

"Yes, I can," she argued back.

"Why would you want to play with boys, anyway?" Frank was irritated. Dragging a girl along. *Geesh!*

Ardell shrugged her shoulders.

Either way, with or without his sister, it was great to get out of the house.

Earl was home and outside. He and Leon were throwing a stick for Leon's dog, Shep, to fetch.

"It's gonna get hot and steamy today," Leon said. "That's what Pappy told me."

Shep brought Leon the stick.

"Good boy," Leon rubbed the dog's head. He held the stick out to Ardell. "Do you want to play fetch with Shep?"

"Hello, Shep," Ardell reached out to scratch his ears. Shep licked her hand, making her giggle. "He likes me."

"Shep likes everyone," said Earl.

Ardell took the stick from Leon and moved away from the boys to play with the dog.

"Hey, Leon, did you bring your gun?" Earl pointed at Frank's holster. "Frank has his."

Leon pulled his out of his pocket.

"Cool, I'll get mine." Earl ran in the house, calling over his shoulder, "I want to be a bad guy." He let the screen door bang shut behind him.

Frank and Leon heard Earl's mom, Betty, tell him, "Not so loud. I finally got the baby to sleep."

"I'll be Roy Rogers," said Leon.

"I can be a bad guy with Earl," Frank said, ready to play with his new guns.

The boys ran all over the yard, hiding behind bushes, by the cellar, even under the porch.

Frank was hiding between the bushes and the house, watching for Leon, his guns drawn, when he realized he hadn't seen his sister for a while. He stood up and looked around.

"Put your hands in the air, and no one gets hurt," Leon came up behind him.

Chapter Five

A Little of Frank's History

"Have you seen Ardell?" Frank ran behind the house, looking over the backyard.

Leon followed him. "Not for a while. She's not playing with Shep. He's asleep on the porch."

The boys ran around to the porch. Earl joined them.

"Maybe she's inside with my mama." Earl opened the screen door and stuck his head in the kitchen. Betty was sitting at the table reading the new Cook Book put

together by the church ladies. "Is Ardell in here?"

"She hasn't been inside at all today," his mom said.

Earl turned back to Frank, shaking his head.

Frank looked around. Next door, Mr. Goins was working with his roses.

Frank ran over to him, starting to panic. "Mr. Goins, have you seen my little sister?" He held his hand up to his chin, about Ardell's height.

"You mean the little girl over yonder playing with Linda Lou and Judy?" he nodded his head, indicating across the street.

Frank whirled around to look behind him. Sure enough, there she was, playing in the neighbor's yard. Linda is the daughter of Beulah Faye, Frank's Sunday school teacher. He ran over to Linda's house.

"Where have you been?" he demanded. "You were supposed to stay at Earl's house and play with Shep!"

"But I want to play with Linda," Ardell pouted. "My friend Judy is visiting, too."

Thinking, Frank shifted from one foot to the other. He looked back and forth between Linda's house and Earl's house. He could easily see from one yard to the other. "Well, okay," he told his sister, coming to a decision. "But stay here! Don't go anywhere else."

"I won't," Ardell promised.

Frank walked back to Earl's where the other boys were sitting on the porch. Being a big brother came with a lot of responsibilities.

"She'll be fine over there," Earl assured him.

"I guess." Frank sat beside Leon, watching the three girls chase a squirrel.

"Where did you move here from?" asked Leon as he stroked Shep's fur.

"We came here by train from California," Frank said.

"California!" Earl exclaimed. "How neat!"

"California is not 'neat'," Leon disagreed, scoffing. "My pappy went to California and came back with polio. Now he wears a big brace on his leg and has to use a cane."

"Really?" Frank turned to Leon. "I think I saw your pappy at Clarkson's store last week."

"Probably," Leon nodded. "He meets his buddies there all the time."

"But, Leon," Earl said, still focused on Frank's having lived in California, "California has beaches. And, don't forget, that's where they make movies and *The Roy Rogers Show*."

Leon shrugged his shoulders, not interested in anything happening in a state that made his pappy sick. "Where's your dad?" he asked Frank.

Now it was Frank's turn to shrug his shoulders. "I don't know. One day he just didn't come home. That's why we moved here. Mom wanted to live near my grandparents."

"That's a hard break," Leon patted Frank on the back.

"Did you always live in California?" Sometimes Earl had such a one-track mind.

"No," Frank shook his head. "We didn't live there long. We've lived in Wisconsin, Arkansas, Kansas, New Mexico and some other states. Mostly in our car."

"Your car!" Earl's eyes widened. "How do you have a bedroom in a car?"

"I don't know. I've never had a bedroom," Frank told them. "Well, we sleep in Mom's bedroom. Do you have a bedroom?" he asked Leon.

"Yep," Leon nodded. "But Mom has to walk through my room to get to her bedroom. Hey, if you came here by train, where's your car?"

"I don't know," Frank told them, again. "Wherever my dad is, probably."

"*Leon!*"

The boys' heads popped up. They looked around, then spotted Leon's pappy. He was by the well behind the hotel.

"I gotta go," he scrambled to his feet. "I have to help Pappy haul water." He took off running.

"I had better get Ardell and head home, too," Frank told Earl.

Chapter Six

The Snake!

"Tomorrow we are going to Hamilton with Shorty's family," Evelyn told the kids as they ate dinner Friday night.

Frank was excited. He had never been to Hamilton, the town five miles west.

"What are we doing in Hamilton?" Frank asked his mom.

"Hamilton has a lot of stores for us to explore. They have horse races and a derby. There's a movie theatre, too. There are all kinds of things to do. Something different each week."

"*Eek! Eek!*" Suddenly, Ardell started screaming. She shoved her plate aside and climbed on the table, pointing at the back door.

They all looked over to see a snake slithering his way across the room.

"Ardell, calm down." Mom crossed the room and picked the snake up below his head. "Quiet down, already. It's only a garter snake. They are harmless."

"It's a snake!" Ardell whimpered.

"We live in a small community surrounded by fields and ponds," she told Ardell. "You might as well get used to seeing a snake every so often."

"But not in the house!"

"No," Mom agreed. "We shouldn't need to see them in the house. Finish eating. I'll be right back." She carried the snake out the back door.

After supper, Mom asked Frank to go outside to get a bucket of water so she could wash the dishes.

Frank usually did this chore every day, but tonight there was a snake out there! He eyed the back door.

"What about the snake, Mom?"

"That snake is long gone," Mom assured him. "Run along, now."

Frank walked to the well cautiously, looking for the snake in the tall grass. He hung the bucket on the hook and started pumping for water. On the way back to the house, he walked even slower. He didn't want to spill any water and have to make another trip to the well tonight!

Chapter Seven

Going to Hamilton

Saturday dawned clear and sunny. A perfect day for the ride to Hamilton. The adults sat in the cab with the baby, Marlene. Frank rode in the bed of the truck with Donna, Sandra, Ardell and Jim.

Shorty drove across the tracks and turned between the churches, stopping in front of Earl's house. Earl was waiting on the front porch.

This was great, Frank thought. He hadn't known Earl was going to town with them. Earl climbed in the bed of the truck and Shorty took off.

"I like riding in the back," Frank told Earl, the breeze blowing his hair straight back. "It's too bad Leon couldn't come with us."

"He's probably already in town," Earl raised his voice as Shorty went faster and the wind picked up. "Him and his mom usually go to town with Mrs. Alborn on Saturday's."

A few miles down the road, Frank pointed to a big building by B Blacktop. "What's that?"

"That's Morning Star Tavern," Earl moved to sit closer to Frank, so they wouldn't have to yell over the wind. "It's for old people, like our parents. They can drink and dance and stuff on the weekends."

"Do your parents go there?"

"No," Earl shook his head. "We drive by there at night, sometimes. There are lots of cars and lights. The music is really loud."

When they reached Hamilton, Shorty parked the truck a block away from the main street.

"Let's all meet back here after the talent show. We'll head home when it's over," Shorty said, turning to walk away.

Evelyn pulled Frank aside. "I'm going to let you go with Earl, since he is familiar with Hamilton. You stay with him, you hear me?"

Frank nodded. "I will."

Mom seemed a little worried about Frank not staying with her for the day. "If you need me, I'll be in one of the stores on the main street."

"Okay, Mom,"

"I'll see you at the talent show," she kissed his forehead. "Be good."

Donna had taken off with a group of girls. The women left with Jim, Sandra and Marlene. Shorty was long gone.

"Come on," Earl tugged on his sleeve. "Let's go."

The boys ran to the main street. It was filled with two rows of cars parked down the center of the road. People were milling around the cars, in the street, up and down the sidewalks, in and out of the stores.

"Hamilton must be huge to have this many people," Frank commented.

"Not really," Earl told him. "Not everyone you see lives here. Some people are like us, coming to town from all over the county and other little towns."

They weaved in and out of the crowd of people on the sidewalk. Frank was amazed at the buildings and cars. He didn't know where to look first.

"Hey," Frank pointed. "There's Leon. *Leon!*" he shouted.

"Leon!" Earl shouted, too.

They caught up with Leon, his mom and Mrs. Alborn. Leon introduced Frank.

"What are you boys planning to do first?" Helen, Leon's mom, asked.

Chapter Eight

Popcorn & Burlap Bags

"Popcorn!" Earl and Leon shouted together.

"I don't have any money," Frank said quietly, disappointed.

Leon's mom heard him. She reached into her pocket book and tried to hand Frank a few coins.

"But…" Frank started to protest.

"Now, none of that," Helen turned his hand over and placed the coins in his palm. "You boys go have a good time."

"Gee. Thank you." Frank stared at the coins, and then gave her a shy smile.

"You're welcome. Go," she sent him after Leon and Earl with a gentle push.

The popcorn stand was a little shack at the intersection of Highway 36 and Highway 13. There was a long line of kids and adults, but it moved fast.

"How many?" the teenage boy working the stand asked.

"Three," said Leon, "and some old maids if you have any, please."

"What is an old maid?" Frank asked Earl.

"It's the kernels that didn't pop," Earl explained.

They moved away from the popcorn shack. Leon held out a much smaller sack than the popcorn bags. "Try them."

Frank tossed a couple in his mouth, crunching them with his teeth. "They're good."

They walked around town, munching their popcorn. There were so many people and so many businesses. They walked by clothing stores, drug stores, barber shops, beauty shops, restaurants, grocery stores, sporting goods stores, and hardware stores. Up and down Davis Street, there were businesses at street level, down in basements and upstairs in the buildings. People young and old called greetings to Leon and Earl. Frank figured they must know almost everyone.

"Pappy's in there, Winslow's," Leon said, pointing to the next building. "Let's go see what he's doing."

Frank and Earl followed him inside. Leon's pappy was sitting with a group of men over in the corner.

"…then the horse took off at a flat out run. Left ole Conner standing there in the middle of the road," one of the men finished his story.

"I'd be madder than an old wet hen," another man said as they all laughed.

"This way." Earl motioned with his hand for them to follow him through a doorway at the back of the store.

"Are we supposed to be in here?" Frank asked, right before he heard voices talking and laughing.

In the back of the building were the feed and crop supplies. Extra pallets held piles of empty feed sacks. Several boys were sitting, bouncing or jumping on the piles.

"Let's have a race." Earl grabbed an empty sack. A few of the other kids grabbed sacks, too. They walked with Earl to the far side of the room.

"This way," Leon pulled Frank to the opposite side of the room.

"What are we doing?" Frank asked as he followed him.

"We're having a feed sack race," Leon said. When Frank still looked puzzled, Leon explained how the game worked. "All the boys down there," he pointed across the room, "will climb into a feed sack. They have to hold it up while they hop across the room to us. Then they get out of the sack and pass it to their partner. The partner has to get in the sack as fast as possible, and then hop back across the room. The first one there wins. Got it?"

"Got it," Frank said, then thought of another question. "What if I fall?"

"You better get up and start hopping!" Leon told him. "It's not a big deal. Someone else might fall, too. It doesn't mean you've lost."

"Okay." *I can do this*, Frank told himself.

"Go," someone yelled.

Earl and three other boys had stepped into the feed sacks. They held the sacks up with their hands about hip level and began jumping toward the line of boys where Frank stood. When they reached the waiting kids, they shucked the sack and handed it to their partner.

Earl tossed his sack to Frank. Frank stepped into the sack as fast as he could. He didn't want to be in last place.

The boy beside him was having trouble. His teammate had been in such a hurry to pass the sack; he had twisted it almost inside out when he pulled it off.

"Go. Go. Hurry," they shouted and cheered. "Faster."

Frank came in third place. Leon thumped him on the back. "Good job."

"That was fun."

"One more time," someone yelled from the other side of the room.

Frank pulled the sack back up to his waist. Now he was experienced. He hopped across the room as fast as he could when the boy gave the signal. The boy ahead of him tripped and fell. Frank hopped around him as he was trying to get up off the floor. He was tangled in

his sack. Frank made it to the other side and passed his bag to Earl.

"Go," Frank yelled with the rest of them. "Go, Earl."

A different team won, but Frank and Earl came in second place.

They put the feed sacks back on the pallets and left the building through one of the open loading bays.

"Do you do this every Saturday?" Frank asked as they merged with the crowd on the sidewalk.

"No," Leon answered him. "We do whatever. Not the same stuff every time we come to town."

"*Boo!*" Someone grabbed Leon's shoulders.

They spun around to see two boys grinning at them.

"Ray Dean, you crud," Leon did a mock punch to the boy's gut. "Where have you been?"

"We got home last night from visiting my grandparents for the last two weeks," Ray Dean told him. He cocked his head toward Frank. "Who is this?"

"This is Frank," Earl said. "He moved into that empty house across from Shorty."

"Hello. I'm Roger," the other boy stretched his hand out to Frank.

Frank couldn't remember ever shaking hands before. As far as he knew it was more of an adult greeting. But, nevertheless, he put his hand in Roger's. Roger squeezed, so Frank squeezed, too.

He must have done the handshake right because Roger gave a curt nod and smiled. "Welcome aboard."

Huh? Frank thought. *Aboard what?* But the other boys had resumed walking. Frank hurried to catch up to them.

Chapter Nine

Get That Turkey!

"What's going on up there?" Earl asked. They worked their way into the crowd of kids gathered in front of Hales Super Market. A man was speaking to the crowd.

"This time, we have released the turkey somewhere here on Davis Street. You are to find him, guide him back here, and you'll get this prize." He held up a bag filled with an assortment of hard candies. "There's only this one prize. We'll give it to one person, or a group can share. And, of course, the winner takes home the turkey. Are you ready?" The kids in the crowd cheered. "On your mark, get set…Go!"

"We can do this." Ray Dean turned to his friends. "Let's work together."

"Yeah," Leon agreed. "That's a big bag of candy. There's plenty to share."

"We are looking for a real turkey?" Frank wanted to make sure he understood correctly. "Won't it fly away?"

"Naw," Roger said. "They've clipped his wings. They usually only do the turkey chase on holidays though. Is today a holiday?"

"Not that I know of," Earl said.

"I don't care," Ray Dean told them. "I've never caught the turkey. This time I want to win!"

"And the winner gets to keep the turkey, too," Roger added.

They started scouring the streets, looking for the turkey. As they worked their way south, Frank spotted his mom.

"Mom," he called to get her attention.

"Frank," she brushed his hair off his forehead. "Are you being good?"

Frank grinned. "I'm having a grand time. Can I tell you about it later? I have to help my friends catch a turkey. Bye," he waved, taking off at a run.

"Did he say turkey?" Mom asked Ardell.

Ardell nodded.

"There he is," Frank heard a girl shout. He looked around. He followed a surge of kids back to the north, making his way through the crowd until he was once again with his friends.

"Stop him!" came another voice.

Frank spotted the turkey running down the sidewalk with two girls chasing him.

"Earl, don't let him get away," Roger yelled.

Ray Dean moved to stand by Earl. The turkey veered away from them. Leon chased the turkey from behind. Frank blocked the turkey's path as Leon and Roger closed in the on other side. The five boys formed a ring, penning the turkey in the middle.

"Squat down, Leon," Roger ordered. "Don't let him get out between your legs. Tighten in everyone." The five boys linked arms.

Walking backwards, trying to watch where you're going, standing close to a person on each side of you, *and* being watched by a crowd of people was not easy. Frank hoped he didn't let the other boys down by being the one that let the turkey get away. Ray Dean wanted to win really bad. And now, so did Frank.

Frank looked behind him. They were making progress, but still had about a block to go.

"Careful, careful," Roger cautioned. "Go slow."

"Yeah," said Ray Dean. "Some other kid will pin him in a heartbeat if we let him get away."

"We can do this," Earl encouraged.

Slowly they worked their way to Hales Super Market. The turkey didn't like being confined. He was trying to fly but couldn't. He ran into Leon, his beak catching Leon's knee.

"Ouch," Leon jerked.

"Don't let him out!" Ray Dean yelled.

"Leon!" Frank warned him when the turkey tried to squeeze between Leon and Roger.

They moved in closer to the turkey, not giving him room to run around.

"Look at these boys," the man announced to the crowd. "We have our winners. Did you see that teamwork in action?" he asked the people.

Another man maneuvered his way into the circle between Frank and Earl. He bagged the turkey with a feed sack, tossed the bag over his shoulder and carried him away. They could hear the turkey throwing a fit.

"Come up here, boys." The man gestured for them to join him in front of the store. "Come get your prize."

Ray Dean accepted the bag of candy, holding it in the air like one would a trophy. A man from the newspaper took a picture. The crowd cheered. Each boy shook the man's hand, telling him thank you. When it was Frank's turn to shake the man's hand, he was glad he had gotten practice doing a handshake with Roger earlier.

The crowd began to disperse.

"Come inside, boys. I'll get you a few empty sacks for dividing your candy."

They followed the man into the store.

Frank looked around. This store wasn't like Clarkson's store. Clarkson's carried a little of everything. Hales mostly sold food.

"Who is that man?" Frank asked Leon.

"That's Mr. Hales," Leon told him. "He owns the store."

Mr. Hales came back with the brown paper sacks. "Come by after the talent show to pick up your turkey," he reminded them. "We'll have him penned up out back of the store."

They told him they would, then left out the front door. The crowd was gone, though the area was still busy with shoppers. Waiting for them were their mothers- Helen, Christine, and Evelyn with Ardell and Jim.

"You finally won," Christine, Ray Dean's mother, squeezed his shoulder.

"I told you I'd catch that turkey someday," he looked up at his mom. "It took all five of us. Did you see? We made a big circle all around him, then made the circle smaller and smaller. He couldn't get away, but he tried to. He pecked Leon, then tried to get out between us, over and over."

"I saw you," his mom answered when Ray Dean stopped to draw a breath.

"I almost fell," Roger admitted. "I didn't see Ann behind me. I bumped into her."

"It was hard walking backwards," Frank agreed.

"That beak was sharp." Leon rolled up his pants leg to examine where the turkey had pecked him. He had a speck of blood right above his knee. "It doesn't hurt," he told his friends.

"So long as you don't eat all the candy at once," Leon's mom told them. "You don't want to upset your stomachs and miss the talent show."

"Here, Mom," Leon handed her his candy. "Wait." He pulled out a piece, then handed the bag back to her. "Can you put mine in your purse? I don't want to spill it or lay it down somewhere and forget it." Earl handed Helen his bag, too.

That was a good idea, Frank thought. He gave his candy to his mom.

Ray Dean's mom took his bag.

"I'm going to put mine in my dad's truck. I'll meet you in front of J.C. Penney's," said Roger.

They had about an hour until the talent show started. They explored a few shops, and then decided to go sit with their parents while they waited for the show to begin. Outside of The Griddle, they ran into Helen. The boys split up. Leon left with his mom to find a place to sit for watching the talent show.

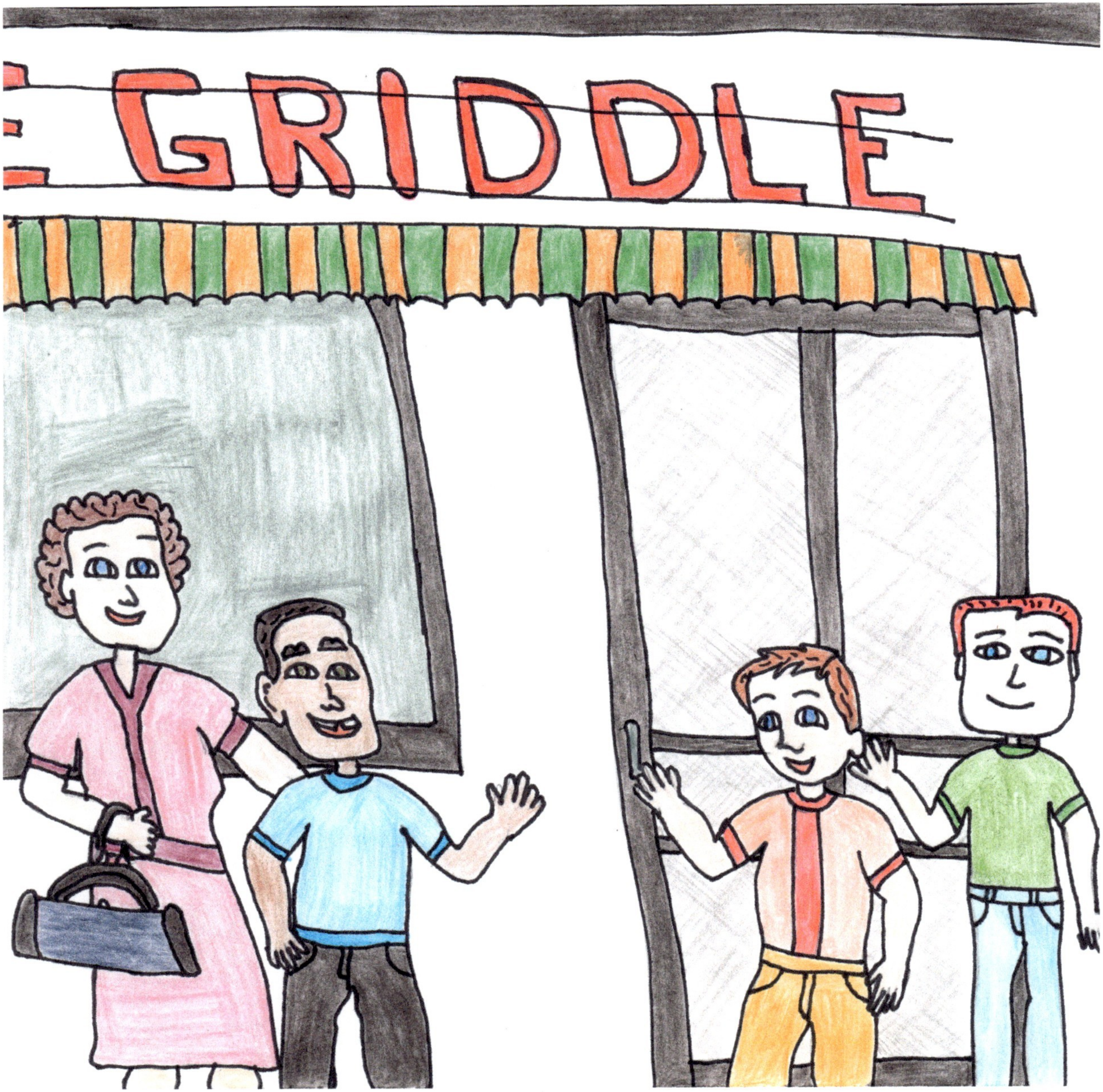
E GRIDDLE

Chapter Ten

The Talent Show

The talent show was in the grassy area between The Hamilton Bank and The Artilla Theater. Frank and Earl found Frank's mom in the crowd of people waiting for the show to start. They plopped down on the blanket she brought from home. Evelyn was emptying the basket of food she had prepared early that morning.

Jim took the carrot his mom held out for him. "I've talked to the other moms about the turkey you won," she told them as she emptied the basket. "Leon's mom is going to take the turkey to their house tonight. Next Sunday, she'll cook the turkey for dinner for you boys. The rest of you will bring a dish to add to the meal."

The plan sounded good to Frank and Earl.

Mom laid out a plate of fried chicken, the potato salad, a bowl with carrots and radishes and unwrapped the towel holding the rolls. The boys helped themselves.

The 'stage' for the talent show was a tractor-trailer rig. The trailer had a set of steps placed at either end for the performers to enter and exit the stage. Banners were tied across the front of the trailer advertising Hamilton Truck and Tractor automotive sales, Hawks Garage used cars, The Hamilton Bank savings bonds, Thomson Hardware's paint sale, Blue Castle's brain sandwiches and gizzards and The Griddle's milkshakes. Stakes were wedged into the frame of the trailer with wire running between them to hold the curtain for the background of the stage.

The talent show began while they were still eating. Frank's favorite act was two teenage girls who played mimes. Frank and Earl laughed and laughed. One girl pretended to kick the other girl but missed. The momentum swung her around in a circle, landing her off balance.

Another act was a couple who sang, "Singing in the Rain."

"They should have sung that song last week," Frank told Earl remembering the leaks in their roof.

"That's for sure," Earl agreed.

Next came a comedian. Frank didn't really understand his jokes. The adults around him laughed, so the man must have been funny.

The last act Frank remembered was the tap dancers. They were really good. It almost sounded like one person tapping instead of six people. They linked arms and tapped in a circle, then back into a straight line.

The next thing Frank remembered was his mom waking him and Earl up for the walk back to Shorty's truck.

"Little Sleepyhead," she jostled his shoulder. "It's time to go home."

Frank woke up enough to walk to Shorty's truck but fell back to sleep after he climbed in the pick-up bed. He even slept through the loud music when they passed Morning Star Tavern on the way home.

Chapter Eleven

Dinner at Leon's

Frank looked forward to the dinner at Leon's house all week. Eating at a friend's house would be another first for him. Though he knew where Leon lived, he'd never been to his house.

The week was fairly uneventful, which made the wait for Sunday dinner seem even longer. He went to church twice, Clarkson's store three times, and played Hide and Seek with Donna, Sandra and Ardell. He even took Ardell to play with her friend Linda.

Finally, they all met at Leon's house. Frank's mom sent mashed potatoes for his contribution to the meal. Roger brought rolls his mom had baked, Ray Dean added corn-on-the-cob, Earl had the apple pie, and Leon's mom cooked dressing with the turkey.

The boys ate until they were stuffed. They practically rolled out the door they were so full!

"I couldn't eat another bite." Roger laid back in the grass, holding his stomach.

"But it was good!" Ray Dean added.

"No, Shep," Leon pushed the dog away. "I'm too full to play fetch."

"Awe, get up, Wilson," Earl told Leon. "We need to use up some of that dinner to make room for the apple pie Mama sent for dessert."

Leon groaned but sat up. They tossed sticks to Shep, then played Cowboys and Indians.

"There's a lightening bug," Frank said, trying to catch it.

"I'll ask Mom for a jar." Leon ran into the house, coming right back with a canning jar.

"Got one," Earl put it in the jar with Frank's.

Frank added another lightening bug, then passed the jar to Ray Dean. It wasn't long before the jar was glowing.

"Boys," Helen called from the doorway. "Time to eat your pie. You'll need to be going home soon."

Roger opened the jar to let the bugs fly away.

The pie was delicious. After dessert, Leon and his friends climbed into the back of his pappy's International for the ride home. Frank was a little disappointed to be the first boy delivered home. But with his full belly, he was ready for bed.

Chapter Twelve

Shorty's Helper

A few days later, Frank was sitting on his front porch when Shorty called out to him. "Come over," he shouted from his ornament shop. "Watch for cars," he added.

Frank stood on the edge of his yard, waiting for a semi-truck and the string of cars behind it to pass. He ran across the highway.

"I'm needing a helper if you're interested," he told Frank.

"Sure," Frank didn't have anything better to do today. "What can I do?"

"Jump up here and sit on this," Shorty patted a board laying across a concrete stand. "I need help balancing this board."

Frank obliged but didn't really pay attention to what Shorty was doing. He was watching the vehicles pulling into the Conoco Station across the way. Some cars were only stopping to get fuel, others would park, and the people would walk inside, probably to eat in the cafe. Another car stopped under the carport and parked. A man left the vehicle and entered one of the motel rooms. What a busy place!

"Okay, you can hop down," Shorty interrupted Frank's musings.

"Could you run over to the hotel and pick up a package for me from Mr. Goins?" Shorty asked. "It's not heavy."

"Sure thing," Frank turned to leave.

"Watch for cars," Shorty reminded him.

Frank safely crossed the highway. At the railroad crossing, he had to wait for a train. Frank could see the crates on the platform the train had delivered. He wanted the train to hurry along. His mom had absolutely forbidden him to walk between the cars when the train was not moving. The train finally started to slowly chug down the tracks, and then gained speed. Frank waited impatiently until the last car had cleared the crossing.

He ran down the road and turned between the churches. As he ran down the sidewalk, he saw Dixie sitting under the tree in her yard petting her kitten. He waved but didn't stop.

He was panting when he stopped under the porch at the hotel. Mr. Goins was sitting in a wooden rocker outside by the front door.

"What can I do for you, son?" he asked. "You didn't lose your sister again, eh?"

"No, sir," Frank took a deep breath. "I'm here to pick up a package for Shorty."

Mr. Goins stopped rocking and stood up. "Follow me. It's in the kitchen."

Frank was excited to see inside the hotel. It is the largest building in Nettleton, as far as he knew.

The front door opened into a foyer. The foyer was a good-sized area. A hallway ran beside a wide staircase. Against the wall of the staircase was a table with a pen and pad of paper laying on a doily. A chair had been placed beside the table. Several paintings were hanging on the wall, but Frank wasn't close enough to see what was in the frames. A long rug ran the length of the hallway. There were doors spaced all down the hallway on both sides.

Frank followed Mr. Goins into the sitting room on the right side of the foyer. An older gentleman was reading a newspaper while listening to the radio. This room had several chairs, small tables, and a settee surrounding a large round rug. And more pictures.

The man briefly looked up from his paper but didn't say anything as they crossed the room to another doorway.

In the kitchen, Mrs. Goins was folding linens at the table. The table was round, with eight chairs. Another staircase was in the corner. They had a big cookstove!

"Here you go," Mr. Goins handed him the package wrapped in brown paper and held in place with burlap twine. It was light as a feather. *Maybe it was full of cotton*, Frank thought.

"That's cotton in there," Mr. Goins told him. "Shorty's wife is needing it for something or other."

Frank was surprised he had guessed right.

"I really like your hotel," Frank told the couple. "It's so big."

"That it is," Mr. Goins agreed. "Follow me. I'll show you something else you might like."

Frank followed Mr. Goins through the rooms once again. As they went through the sitting room, Frank noticed the gentlemen who had been reading the paper had fallen asleep. He was snoring.

Mr. Goins closed the front door behind them. He turned and gestured to the doorknob. "Turn the knob, son."

Frank grabbed the knob, turning it to the right to open the door.

"Not that way," Mr. Goins stopped him. "Try the other direction."

Frank was beginning to think he was being teased. What if Mrs. Goins yelled at him? Mr. Goins was still waiting for him to follow his instructions. Cautiously, Frank turned the knob to the left.

Uurrrhhh. The door buzzed. Frank let go of the knob as though it was a hot potato!

Mr. Goins laughed. "Bet that won't make Ma too happy."

Frank believed Mr. Goins was a little bit of a prankster.

"Go ahead," he waved at the knob. "Give it another turn. In for a penny, in for a pound, I always say."

Frank knew he probably shouldn't, but it was fun. He turned the knob. *Uurrrhhh*. He giggled.

Frank picked up Shorty's package, thanked Mr. Goins and left.

Earl was outside his house when Frank started his trip back to Shorty's.

"Guess what?" Earl asked, crossing the yard from his porch to meet Frank on the sidewalk.

"What?" Frank returned, though he should have tried to guess since he had guessed the cotton right. He could be on a good guessing streak!

"We're moving Saturday," Earl told him, grinning.

Frank wasn't sure how to respond. He never liked moving, but Earl was grinning. "Are you excited?"

"*Duh*," Earl said, making it sound like 'of course, who wouldn't be excited to move?' "It'll be different, that's for sure. I've always lived in this house. I was born here, you know."

"I didn't. That's great news," Frank told him. "The move, I mean." He couldn't imagine having lived in the same place for years and years. He had lived in so many places. Frank would love to live in the same house for years, but Earl was looking forward to moving because he had always lived in the same house. "I have to get this package to Shorty. I'll talk to you later, okay?"

Shorty was surprised when Frank returned with the package so soon. "Maybe I forgot to tell you there wasn't any need to hurry?"

"Oh," Frank said. He had hurried because he didn't want to keep Shorty waiting. "It's all good."

"Here," Shorty fished a coin out of his pocket and flipped it to Frank.

Frank caught it between his palms.

"Have a game on me," he tilted his head toward the cafe. "You earned it."

"Thanks, Shorty." Frank put the nickel in his pocket. Maybe the pinball machine was available. Sometimes there was a line of kids waiting their turn.

"See you later."

"Thanks for the help," Shorty called after him. "And watch for cars."

"I know," Frank called over his shoulder.

Chapter Thirteen

Mom's Good News

Frank ran home to tell his mom about his nickel and how he'd earned it.

"Look, Mom," he held it out to show her.

"Go back and close the door, please," she ordered.

"I did shut the door," he mumbled as he did what he was told.

He shut the door, again, but as he turned away the door creaked open. He tried one more time. Still it wouldn't stay shut!

"Mom," he called, "the door won't stay shut."

Drying her hands on her apron, Evelyn came into the living room to check for herself. Sure enough, the wood had swelled and wouldn't fit the frame.

"You're right," she said. "I'll take care of it. Now, what were you trying to tell me?"

"Never mind," Frank knew his mom was busy. "I'll tell you at dinner. Can I go play pinball?"

"Sure, honey," Mom was fiddling with the door. "Be home in time for dinner."

Frank used the back door, then ran across the yard to the café. As it turned out, there was a group of older boys, including Jack and Pete, surrounding the pinball machine, watching one of their friends play.

Frank returned his nickel to his pocket and went outside. He could see Aunt Ada working in her garden. Ardell was helping her. At least, he hoped she was helping and not hindering. He decided he'd better go check on his little sister.

As he approached, he could see Ardell holding a basket filled with lettuce, corn and radishes.

"Can you give that to your mom for me?" Aunt Ada asked Ardell. "Tell her there's no hurry to give the basket back."

"I will," Ardell promised.

"Do you need help, Aunt Ada?" Frank asked.

"No," she told him. "I'm about done for the day. Thank you for the offer."

"I could help you water tomorrow, if you want."

"That is an offer I might take you up on, young man," she tweaked his nose.

"I'll come over after breakfast," Frank said.

"Don't rush your eating."

"I won't," he said.

Later, sitting at the dinner table, Frank told his mom all about his day.

"I have some news, too," Mom told her kids when Frank was finished.

"Is it about the baby?" Ardell asked, getting excited.

"No," Mom smiled. "We need to wait a couple more months to meet the baby. But…" she left them in suspense while she took a drink of water.

"Mo-o-om," Frank tried rushing her to give them the news.

"What, Mom? What?" Ardell was bouncing in her seat.

"The good news is," she resumed, "we're moving."

"No!" Frank shouted, immediately upset. "That's not good news. I like living in Nettleton."

Ardell's lip started to quiver. She had tears in her eyes. "Not again."

"Hold on," Mom's voice took on a soothing tone, "I told you it was good news." She brushed away Ardell's tears. "We are moving to where Earl is living. We will move into that house as soon as Earl's family gets moved to their new house. And…"

"What? And what?" Frank scooted to the edge of his chair, his mood swinging uphill. He was already smiling.

"*And* we are buying the house."

Obviously, this last bit of news was important, but Frank didn't understand.

"That means," their mom explained, "that we will live there for a long, long time."

Frank jumped up, whooping. He grabbed Ardell's hands, and they danced around the kitchen. Jim didn't know why they were dancing, but he wanted to dance with them.

Frank had never been so excited in his whole seven years. He couldn't wait to tell his friends. He had to tell his Uncle Lindy, too.

Chapter Fourteen

That Odd Little Man

As it turned out, Uncle Lindy already knew they were moving, which sort of burst Frank's bubble. But not for long! Uncle Lindy had been working with his mom for a couple of weeks to buy the house.

"You," he clamped his hand on Frank's shoulder, "were how we were able to buy the house in the first place."

"I was?" Frank tried to think back on his actions. "What did I do?"

"Remember the day you came home, telling us Earl was moving?"

"Oh," Frank's eyes widened. He remembered that day.

"Your mom and I went to see Mr. Millet, who owns that house, the very next day," Uncle Lindy explained.

Frank couldn't stop grinning. "I can't wait to tell my friends," Frank told his uncle.

Frank was so excited about moving. He'd moved a lot of times in his seven years of life, but this was the first time he could remember actually looking forward to moving. It was hard waiting almost a week. Now he understood how Earl felt.

The next day he saw Sam, Aunt Ada's youngest son, sitting on the front porch.

"What are you doing?" Frank asked Sam.

"I'm trying to get this radio tuned," Sam had the radio taken apart. The pieces were strung all around him. "See this?" He used his screwdriver to indicate a nub with a missing dial. The dial was with the other parts scattered across the porch boards. "That won't turn easy. It keeps catching."

Frank only paid a little attention to Sam's project. "Did you hear we're moving?"

"You are?" That got Sam's attention. "When?"

"In a few days," Frank told him, grinning from ear to ear. "We're moving into Earl's house." In case Sam misunderstood, Frank clarified. "The house he lives in now. He's moving to a new house, then we get to move to his old house."

"I bet you will like living there," Sam said, bending back over his radio. "We won't be neighbors once you move," he pointed out.

Frank hadn't considered that aspect. He liked living near Aunt Ada. Ardell and his mom did, too. Upon consideration, though, the new house was still a good deal.

"We won't be far away," he reassured Sam.

Two days before their big moving day, Ardell had her friend Linda over to play while Beulah Faye went shopping. After lunch, Beulah Faye returned the favor by watching Ardell and Jim while Evelyn shopped.

Frank went with his mom to help carry any boxes Nathan and Bung might have on hand. They needed them for packing, and they needed to get a few groceries and pick up any mail that might be waiting for them at the post office.

Bung had started letting Frank retrieve popped off lids out of the Coca-Cola machine when he showed an interest in starting a collection last week. He was pulling them out of the bin when he noticed a funny-looking man enter the store.

The man was short, like a twelve-year-old boy. He wore a weird hat that looked like a lamp shade; his skin was yellowish and his clothes rumpled and dirty.

Frank followed him to the meat counter in the back of the store. Nathan was cutting the man an order of sliced ham. The guy sure did talk funny. Frank couldn't understand a word he said, even though he could tell the man was speaking English.

He ran over to his mom, tugging on her sleeve. "Mom, who is that?" he pointed to the funny little guy.

"Don't point," Mom scolded him. "It isn't polite." She turned to see where he was pointing. She lowered her voice. "That's one of the Chinese workers from the railroad east of town. You stay away from them."

"Why?" Frank wanted to know.

"They drink a lot," she whispered, turning back to her shopping list. "You mind me, now."

Chapter Fifteen

Moving Day

Moving day had arrived! Earl's dad had given Evelyn the key to the house yesterday, as they had finished moving all their belongings into their new house. Frank, Ardell and Jim had helped their mom empty the cabinets and gather their clothes after breakfast. The boxes they had gotten from Clarkson's store were filled and stacked by the front door.

As it happened, moving day was also the same day the women of the WPFA were throwing a baby shower for Frank's mom in the big, brick feed store.

"This will work out fine," Uncle Lindy told his sister. "You don't need to be doing a lot of lifting in your condition. You and Ardell have a good time at the party. The boys and I will round up a little help. We'll have you moved in no time. Come with me, Frank." Uncle Lindy picked up Jim and carried him outside. Frank followed his uncle.

Shorty was happy to help with the move. He backed his truck up to the front door and they started loading the furniture. When they couldn't fit anymore in the truck, they drove to the new house.

Frank hadn't been inside the house, only outside playing in the yard. He jumped out of the bed of the truck before Shorty and his uncle had time to open their doors. He clambered up the steps and across the porch. The front door opened into the kitchen with a bedroom and living room downstairs. At the top of the stairs was an area to use as a bedroom with another room leading off to the west. Exploring done, Frank ran back downstairs to carry the smaller items into the house while Uncle Lindy and Shorty took care of the bigger furniture.

They hadn't acquired many possessions. After three loads, they had everything moved to their new house. Uncle Lindy had Frank help with the unpacking. They put away the dishes while Shorty worked upstairs.

"Your mom will probably move everything to where she wants it, but at least she won't have to do it immediately," Uncle Lindy told Frank.

"Probably," Frank agreed with his uncle, placing their dish towels in a drawer. Jim was running in circles around the kitchen table.

"Are you ready for your surprise?" Shorty asked as he came down the stairs.

"A surprise for me?"

"For all you kids, really," Uncle Lindy told him. "But, as our good helper today, you get to see the surprise first."

Frank followed the men upstairs. When his uncle moved to the side, Frank saw a bed. Jim tried to run around Frank, but Uncle Lindy scooped him into his arms.

"This is Ardell's room," Uncle Lindy told him, then crossed the room to the door on the right side of the room. "Here is the room you will share with Jim."

"Really?" Frank's eyes got big as saucers. "Our very own bedrooms? And a bed?" He ran across to the room that would be for the boys.

Sure enough, there was a big bed for him and his brother to share. They had a dresser and a closet. All for them.

Shorty had stacked the boxes with Frank and Jim's clothes in the corner of the room. There was a rug in the middle of the floor, but no curtains, yet.

Frank turned around and hugged Uncle Lindy around the waist. "Thank you. It's the bestest surprise ever!"

"We'll be downstairs," Uncle Lindy gave his hair a ruffle. "When you're ready, we'll go over to the baby shower and help your mom bring her gifts home from the party."

"I'll be down in a minute," Frank told them. He heard them clomp down the stairs. He wanted to stay in his new bedroom forever. His very own bedroom! Of course, he had to share with Jim, but that was okay, too.

Frank walked down the stairs feeling happier than he ever had in his whole life. He had lots of friends, great neighbors, and a house to live in for years and years. Could life get any better? There was no doubt in Frank's mind, he had found his true home.

THE END